FLEATECTIVES

CASE OF THE SLIMY BANK ROBBERS

Look out for more

FLEATECTIVES

adventures

CASE OF THE STOLEN NECTAR

CASE OF THE MISSING GLOW-WORMS

CASE OF THE KIDNAPPED MANTIS

FLEATECTIVES

CASE OF THE SLIMY BANK ROBBERS

JONNY ZUCKER

ILLUSTRATED BY CHRIS JEVONS

SCHOLASTIC

First published in the UK in 2015 by Scholastic Children's Books
An imprint of Scholastic Ltd
Euston House, 24 Eversholt Street,
London, NW1 1DB, UK
Registered office: Westfield Road, Southam, Warwickshire, CV47 0RA
SCHOLASTIC and associated logos are trademarks and/
or registered trademarks of Scholastic Inc.

Text copyright © Jonny Zucker, 2015
Illustrations copyright © Chris Jevons, 2015

The rights of Jonny Zucker and Chris Jevons to be identified as the author and
illustrator of this work have been asserted by them.

Cover illustration © Chris Jevons, 2015

ISBN 978 1407 13697 4

A CIP catalogue record for this book is available from the British Library.

Printed and bound by CPI Group (UK) Ltd, Croydon, CR0 4YY
Papers used by Scholastic Children's Books
are made from wood grown in sustainable forests.

1 3 5 7 9 10 8 6 4 2

www.scholastic.co.uk

For Fleathfield and Bitemoor
Primary Schools

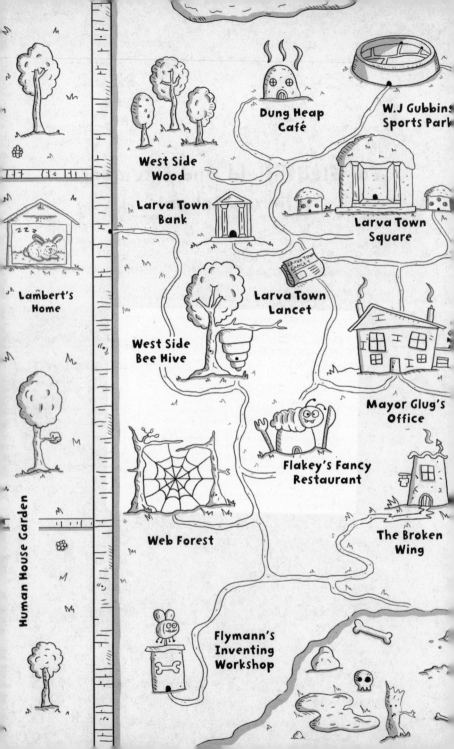

Human House Garden

Lambert's Home

West Side Wood

Dung Heap Café

W.J Gubbins Sports Park

Larva Town Bank

Larva Town Square

Larva Town Lancet

West Side Bee Hive

Mayor Glug's Office

Flakey's Fancy Restaurant

Web Forest

The Broken Wing

Flymann's Inventing Workshop

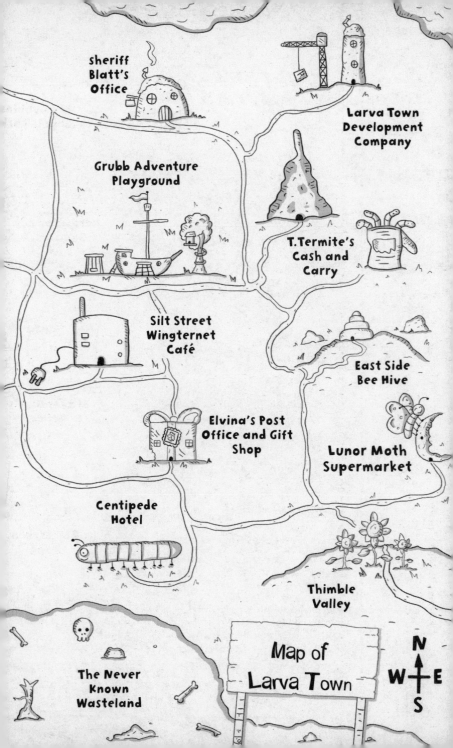

CHAPTER 1

It was early evening and Larva Town's crime-crushing Fleatectives – Buzz and Itch – were relaxing in a muddy pool of slime. Buzz was floating on a leaf, reading a book about famous worm art thieves. Itch was holding a home-made bark bow, getting ready to fire his first dandelion-stalk arrow.

"Watch this!" shouted Itch. He pulled the arrow back and let it go. It soared into the air. "It works!" cried Itch proudly.

At that moment, a gust of wind swirled through the air, spun the arrow round and sent it hurtling back in Itch's direction.

"Disaster!" cried Itch, wading through the oozing pool with the arrow racing after him. When it was nearly upon him, he dropped his bow and dived head first under the surface. The arrow missed him by a few millimetres.

Dribbling and gurgling slime, he raised his head and was about to start looking for the bow when a very loud shriek echoed around him.

"Oh no, Buzz!" gasped Itch, wiping oozing drops of slime out of his antennae. "Did my arrow hit you?"

"No," replied Buzz. "It's not me who's shouting, it's him!"

Itch followed Buzz's eyes and saw a beefy green dragonfly zooming past the pool. He stopped for a second and pulled up a rock. After having a quick look under it he yelled, "NOTHING THERE!" before dropping the rock and racing onwards.

"Isn't that Van Punchem, the head of security at Larva Town Bank?" asked Itch.

"Yes," nodded Buzz. "It looks like

something fishy is up."

"But there are no fish round here," frowned Itch, searching the slime for any sea creatures.

Buzz slid off his leaf and jumped as quickly as he could after the dragonfly, with Itch squelching behind him. Van Punchem was up ahead, flying into trees, diving into bushes and kicking aside stones, all the while screaming and wailing. He was moving remarkably fast and covering lots of ground.

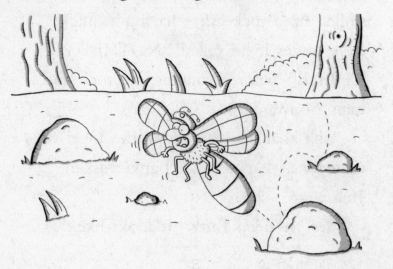

FLEATASTIC FACT:
The Globe Skimmer dragonfly lives for less than a year, but in that time it can fly _eleven thousand miles_ back and forth across the Indian Ocean!

The Fleatectives finally caught up with him.

"Hey, Mr Punchem," said Itch, "what's got your tail in such a twist?"

Van Punchem stopped and turned round to face the Fleatectives. Up close, his eyes looked really big. "When I went to unlock the bank for its evening opening hours, I discovered the place had been totally cleaned out," groaned Van Punchem.

"You must have great cleaners," smiled

5

Itch. "Is it lovely to see the bank looking so neat and tidy?"

"No," sighed Buzz, "'cleaned out' means stolen. He means the bank's money wasn't there."

"Thieves broke into the vault – the special room where we keep all the Bug Notes – and took *everything*," wailed Van Punchem. "Now the bank has got NO money AT ALL! I've searched everywhere but I can't find it. Plus, I have no idea how the robbers got in. There's only one door to the bank and one door leading to the vault, and they were both locked. I'm the only one who has the keys."

"But that's terrible!" exclaimed Itch. "If there's no money how will anyone buy things?"

"No one will be able to buy ANYTHING," replied Van Punchem.

"The whole of Larva Town could be destroyed if we don't find that money."

He burst out crying.

"There, there," said Buzz, putting a claw on the dragonfly's back. "Why don't you take us to the bank and let us have a look at the crime scene? We're not called the Fleatectives for nothing."

Ten minutes later, the three of them arrived at a large rectangular stone building with the words LARVA TOWN BANK printed above the entrance. Van Punchem got out a key and opened the door. "You two go inside and take a look around," he said, pulling a pair of binoculars out from under his wing. "I'm going to search outside and see if I can find any clues."

The Fleatectives entered the bank and saw two gleaming red service counters on the right and a row of silver cash machines on the left. Straight ahead was the bank's enormous metal vault.

"I wonder how they got in?" murmured Buzz, looking around and seeing that all of the bank's windows were firmly closed and locked.

"This must be the work of those two

fiendish criminals: The Painted Lady and her horrible sidekick, Crustman," shivered Itch.

The exquisitely decorated butterfly and her woodlouse assistant had never been caught for any crimes. But whenever something bad happened in Larva Town, they always topped the Fleatectives' list of potential suspects.

"Did you just mention The Painted Lady and Crustman?" shouted Van Punchem, racing into the bank.

The Fleatectives nodded.

"Well, I've just seen them through my binoculars," panted Van Punchem. "Crustman is pushing a large wheelbarrow that's covered by a blanket."

"Aha!" declared Itch. "The Bug Notes must be in that wheelbarrow!"

"You stay here, Mr Punchem, while we

go and nab those two villains!" shouted Buzz. He and Itch turned round quickly and sprinted out of the building.

Can you solve these word jumbles?

1. STAN CRUM

2. ZIZ TAD BUNCH

3. BETS O NUG

4. CHAMP NEVUN

5. PANDA YET LID

6. BOW VAN TAR LANK

Answers at the back of the book

CHAPTER 2

"At last we're going to catch those two red-handed!" yelled Itch, as he and Buzz raced after their suspects. "There's no way they'll be able to wriggle out of this one."

The Fleatectives sped down a stony path and swerved round the corner. There were The Painted Lady and Crustman. He was pushing a green wheelbarrow covered by a large blue woollen blanket. They were whispering to each other.

"Stop right there!" commanded Buzz. "We know you have stolen goods and we know where you're keeping them."

"Is that right?" purred The Painted Lady,

her voice sounding silky yet menacing. "And where might these 'goods' be exactly?"

"You can't pull the wool blanket over our eyes," cried Itch. He jumped over to the wheelbarrow and whisked away the blanket.

But the wheelbarrow wasn't stuffed with Bug Notes. Instead, the whole thing was filled with kids' mini insect action figures. There was Super Red Ant, the Kung Fu Stick Insect and Earwig Butt Kicker.

Crustman's cheeks went a very deep shade of raspberry red.

"Kids' mini insect action figures?" said Buzz, looking very confused.

"He collects them," said The Painted Lady sharply. "I've told him that perhaps he's a tiny bit too old for them but he refuses to give up."

"They're fun," croaked Crustman. "And you can make them fight each other!"

"Right," nodded Itch with disappointment. "We got you mixed up with some hideous bank-robbing villains. It's an easy mistake to make if you insist on pushing wheelbarrows around."

"Stay out of our way," hissed The Painted Lady, "and we'll stay out of yours."

Buzz and Itch shivered as Crustman carefully replaced the blanket and slunk away with his butterfly companion.

In a few minutes the Fleatectives were back inside the bank. *Gone off to search for the money*, Van Punchem had written on a noticeboard. *Left the vault open for you.*

Buzz and Itch walked past the large open metal door leading into the vault. The vault was a large circular room with no windows. "Van Punchem was right," said Itch.

"There are no Bug Notes in here – not a single one," nodded Buzz.

But Itch had spotted something. "Hey, check this out," he said, picking a ripped piece of paper up off the floor. There were three words on it:

"The crooks must have dropped it," said Buzz.

"Why would frying toads at night be part of their plan?" asked Itch.

"Maybe that's what they ate before they set out to perform the crime," said Buzz, kneeling down to take a closer look at the vault's stone floor tiles.

"What are you doing?" scolded Itch. "We're not floor inspectors, we're crime-crushers! We have clues to search for."

"I think I might have just found one," said Buzz, using all of his strength and pushing a floor tile to one side. Beneath it was a small hole. Itch knelt down next to his fellow Fleatective. Together they peered into the darkness below.

Buzz pulled a candle out from his thorax and lit it. Then he gently lowered himself into the blackness.

"Are you crazy?" gasped Itch. "There could be anything down there – monsters or ghosts or creatures with three heads and extra-large teeth."

Buzz reached up, grabbed one of Itch's legs and pulled him down into the hole.

Buzz held the candle above his head and the Fleatectives examined their new surroundings.

"So this is how they got in," whispered Itch. "They dug a tunnel."

"Come on," said Buzz, "let's see where it goes."

The candle threw strange shadows on the tunnel wall. Itch whimpered in fear and clung on to Buzz's shoulder as they stepped forwards. They looked on the floor for signs of Bug Notes but there were none.

The tunnel wasn't very long and a short while later they saw a light up ahead. They walked on and saw that the

light was coming from a hole above their
heads.

"This must be the start of the tunnel,"
said Buzz.

The Fleatectives pulled themselves up and out of the hole and found themselves standing on a lush patch of grass, a short distance away from the bank. In front of them were two delicate-looking, spotty ladybirds, each one holding a very fashionable handbag.

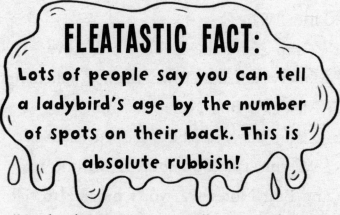

FLEATASTIC FACT:

Lots of people say you can tell a ladybird's age by the number of spots on their back. This is absolute rubbish!

"And who are you two?" enquired Buzz. The ladybirds jumped in surprise.

"I'm Lilac and she's Mauve," said the first one.

"No you're not," said Itch, "you're both red with black spots."

"I think those are their names," cut in Buzz.

"Oh," said Itch. "I love your handbags. They're very cool."

"Have either of you seen anyone climbing out of this tunnel?" asked Buzz.

"Apart from you two, no one," replied Lilac. "Why?"

"I'm afraid there's been a massive robbery at Larva Town Bank," replied Itch. "All of its Bug Notes are gone."

"But that's terrible!" gasped Mauve. "We run a fashion shop. If no one has any Bug Notes we won't be able to sell anything and will be forced to close. Can the crime be solved?"

"Of course the crime can be solved," said a fruity voice. A cockroach appeared with a shiny white "S" painted on his shell.

"Sheriff Blatt," said Itch sulkily. "What brings you here?"

"I heard about the bank robbery," replied the sheriff. "As Larva Town's official law enforcer, I'll take things from here. My eagle eyes will be sure to spot the villain. Of course I'll have to watch the insect TV show, *Butterfly Bank Raids,* before I get started, but then nothing will stop me."

"We got to the crime scene first," snapped Itch. "It's our case."

"You're amateurs and I'm a professional," said Blatt firmly, "so keep out of this."

"Well, I hope you find the robbers," said Mauve. "It's the only way we'll save our shop."

And with that she and Lilac hurried off, clutching their handbags.

"It's time for you two to move on," said Blatt, waving the Fleatectives away.

"We're going," said Itch, "but you won't solve this mystery, Sheriff Blatt. We will."

The Fleatectives turned and headed home, talking about the case. They needed to find out who had nabbed the money, what had they done with it, and whether or not there was a chance of getting it back.

Home was a rabbit called Lambert. Lambert was big and white, and she slept a very great deal.

The Fleatectives were always amazed by this because she never seemed to do anything. They both took a quick bite of her when they arrived.

"Ouch!" she cried, opening one eye. "How many times have I told you not to bite me?"

"Come on, Lambert," said Buzz. "We only do it when we're hungry, and anyway, we need some help with a case."

The Fleatectives climbed up Lambert's back.

Lambert yawned and closed her eye. "What is it?" she said, stretching.

"There's been a major burglary at the Larva Town Bank," replied Itch. "Some insect or insects have taken all of the Bug Notes, and I mean ALL of them."

Both of Lambert's eyes suddenly snapped open. "I may have some useful information for you about this case," she said.

"Really?" asked Buzz.

"Yes," nodded Lambert. "I think I know who your criminal might be."

Which tunnel leads to the Larva Town Bank?

A

B

C

Flakey's Fancy Restaurant

Larva Town Bank

Lunor Moth Supermarket

Answers at the back of the book

CHAPTER 3

"Who is it?" demanded Itch, hopping from side to side in excitement.

"There's a sly old dung beetle called Snoop Crenshaw," replied Lambert. "He runs the Larva Town Development Company."

"Couldn't he run something with a shorter name?" asked Itch.

"That's the company that builds all of the new flats, houses and shopping centres in Larva Town," said Buzz. "Snoop Crenshaw is in charge of it."

"Correct," said Lambert. "I've heard he's been having lots of money troubles recently.

It sounds like he's run out of cash."

"So a bank robbery would make perfect sense," said Buzz thoughtfully.

"Absolutely," nodded Lambert, turning on her side.

"I think we should go to bed," said Buzz, looking up at the pale crescent moon. "In the morning we'll go and check out Mr Crenshaw."

But Itch was already fast asleep and snoring softly.

Buzz sighed and snuggled deeper into Lambert's fur. It had been an eventful few hours and the Fleatectives needed some rest.

When Buzz got up the next morning, Itch was standing on the ground a short distance away from Lambert. He was shaking his abdomen and swinging his head round and round.

"Er ... what are you doing?" asked Buzz.

"I'm trying to fly," panted Itch. "That way I'll get to Snoop Crenshaw in record time."

Buzz grabbed Itch's antennae and made him stop. "How many times do I have to tell you?" cried Buzz. "We're fleas, Itch. We can't fly. We jump."

Itch looked crestfallen for a moment, but then he remembered the morning's plan and quickly cheered up. "Shall we go now?" he asked.

Buzz nodded and after taking a quick nibble of Lambert, they set off.

The Larva Town Development Company

was in the north-east part of town and on the way they passed the Grubb Adventure Playground. Two dad grubs were standing by the play equipment as their kids fought over who could eat a patch of mildew on the seat of a swing.

"If there's no money in town, how am I going to get my grass suits cleaned?" one of the dads was saying.

"I'll clean them for you if you give me a ticket for the next Tapeworm Terrors concert," replied the second one.

"That's ridiculous!" snapped the first one. "A Tapeworm Terrors ticket is worth far more than a session of grass-suit cleaning."

"No it's not!" shouted the second one. "Grass-suit cleaning is a very time-consuming job."

"That's what happens when there's no money in town," gulped Buzz as the

Fleatectives hurried past the playground. "If we don't solve this case soon there's going to be a whole lot of trouble round here, with insects arguing about how to pay each other for things."

Half an hour later they arrived at the Larva Town Development Corporation. This was a tall building with a semi-circle of mud for a roof. Standing next to it was a giant crane. This had a sign hanging off it stating:

WARNING!

STAY AWAY FROM THIS CRANE
OR YOU MIGHT HAVE A VERY
UNPLEASANT AND NASTY ACCIDENT
AND THE LTDC DOESN'T HAVE
ENOUGH PLASTERS FOR EVERYONE

"I should have brought my own plasters," muttered Itch.

They walked up to the building. The front door was open.

"Anyone around?" called out Buzz.

There was no reply.

"Maybe we should just go home," said Itch, looking around nervously. "If Snoop Crenshaw is the Bug Note thief, he might attack us because we're trying to solve the crime."

"We're going in," said Buzz firmly. Itch gulped and followed Buzz inside.

They stepped into a narrow, dimly lit

corridor. They crept forwards slowly and searched for clues.

"Check this out," whispered Buzz. He pointed to a notebook that was lying on a table. Under a heading "HOW MUCH MONEY DO I HAVE?" was the figure "0".

"It's him," hissed Itch. "Snoop Crenshaw has no money, so he must be the bank robber."

They passed a tall bark worktop and reached another open door. Moving through it, they entered a huge rectangular room. There were building materials everywhere: lengths of branches, piles of stones, lines of mud bricks and pots of buttercup concrete mix. Pictures of homes for bees and wasps and worms and ants covered the walls.

"Wow!" said Itch, "Snoop Crenshaw

must make houses for most of the insects in Larva Town."

FLEATASTIC FACT:
There are between six million and ten million different types of insects!

On the left wall was a large cupboard, and sticking out between its two sliding doors was a selection of white pieces of paper.

"Bug Notes!" gasped Itch. "We've solved the crime already. We're Super Fleatectives!"

"Let's get them out and load them into a sack or something," nodded Buzz. "Then we can arrest Mr Crenshaw and take all of the loot to Van Punchem. He'll be delighted."

"We may even get medals from Mayor Glug," beamed Itch. "We could be on insect TV!"

They moved forwards and took one of the cupboard doors each. "OK," whispered Buzz. "On the count of three."

Itch nodded.

"One," said Buzz.

"Two," said Buzz.

"Three," said Itch.

They pulled open the doors and a gigantic flood of paper cascaded down on them.

"HELP!" screamed Itch. "We're going to drown!"

Help Buzz and Itch find their way to the Larva Town Development Corporation.

START

FINISH

Answers at the back of the book

CHAPTER 4

Buzz and Itch flailed their arms and tried to scream as the paper kept pouring on top of them. It was a deadly paper river.

Two claws suddenly grabbed Buzz and Itch and lifted them out from the falling paper. They gasped for air and were gently lowered on to the ground. They discovered it was a large brown dung beetle that had saved them.

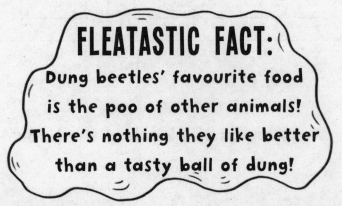

FLEATASTIC FACT: Dung beetles' favourite food is the poo of other animals! There's nothing they like better than a tasty ball of dung!

"Snoop Crenshaw?" asked Buzz.

The dung beetle nodded.

"In the name of the law, we arrest you!" cried Itch, puffing out his chest.

"Er . . . Itch," said Buzz.

"We will take all of this loot you stole and return it to the bank."

"Er . . . Itch," said Buzz a little louder.

"You will be locked in jail and—"

"IT'S NOT THE STOLEN MONEY!" shouted Buzz.

"Huh?" said Itch. He stared down at the paper, noticing immediately that there wasn't a Bug Note in sight.

"These papers are all of the bills I haven't paid yet," said Snoop. "Building insect homes is a very expensive business."

"So you *have* run out of money!" said Itch. "That makes you the number-one suspect for the robbery."

"Last week I didn't have any money," said Snoop, "but three days ago, my rich Uncle Gremlin visited town. I told him about my money troubles and he gave me a whole load of money so that I could pay my bills and carry on building houses."

"Have you ever seen this note before?" asked Itch, holding up the ripped paper with the words FRI, NIGHT and TOAD.

"I'd never fry toad," said Snoop. "It would taste disgusting!"

"So you're not the thief?" asked Itch, scratching the top of his head.

"Absolutely not," replied Snoop, "but I may have some information for you about the bank job."

"And what's that?" asked Buzz.

Snoop lowered his voice. "There's whisper travelling round town that an old wasp called Maxi saw something near the bank around the time of the theft."

"And how is the whisper travelling?" asked Itch.

"What did he see?" demanded Buzz, ignoring his crime-crushing partner.

"I don't know," said Snoop. "Apparently he'll only talk if someone pays him."

"PAYS HIM!" blurted out Itch. "We're real, top-of-the-range, full-time crime-crushers – we don't pay for info."

"In this case we might need to," murmured Buzz.

"Where does this Maxi guy hang out?" asked Itch.

"At Flakey's Fancy Restaurant," replied Snoop. "He'll probably be there now."

"Thanks, Mr Crenshaw," called Buzz, taking Itch by the claw and leading him back towards the door. "We'll be in touch if we need anything else."

"Do you think Snoop Crenshaw was lying?" asked Itch as they jumped towards Flakey's. "Could he be the thief?"

"I'm not sure I believe his story about his Uncle Gremlin giving him all of that money," replied Buzz. "And although we didn't find the Bug Notes, he could be hiding them somewhere."

A few minutes later, the Fleatectives reached Flakey's Fancy Restaurant. This was blue and dome shaped with a massive model of a goofy-looking worm on the roof and a giant pink knife and fork on either side.

Flakey's Fancy Restaurant

It was bright inside with a series of shiny oval tables and a sparkly serving counter on the right. Three ants on mini-Rollerblades were scooting across the floor delivering orders to customers.

It was incredibly noisy at the counter, as many insects had already run out of money.

"I'll give you some wing hairs if you give me a Nectar Cola!" shouted a small bee.

"Can I trade one of my legs for some Grit Crisps?" demanded a stick insect.

"We need to find those missing Bug Notes quickly," said Itch, looking at this mad scene, "or else things will get REALLY bad in Larva Town."

At the furthest table sat an elderly wasp. He was staring out of the window and sipping from a thin cup of something warm and frothy. The Fleatectives approached him.

"Are you Maxi?" asked Buzz.

"I may be."

"That's crazy," said Itch, "you must

know who you are. Even my cousin, Dorkin, knows who he is, and he's only one year old!"

"All right, I am Maxi."

"Good," said Buzz. He and Itch sat down on either side of the wasp.

"We've heard you saw something suspicious near Larva Town Bank yesterday," said Buzz. "Around the time of the robbery?"

"I did," nodded Maxi. "But I won't say a word until someone gets me something to eat."

Buzz sighed and pulled out his last couple of Bug Notes. "Buy yourself some food and then talk."

And so it was that five minutes later, Maxi was stuffing chalk fritters, soil pancakes and dead grass omelettes into his mouth, washing the whole lot down with a large mug of leaf juice.

"So go on, then," said Itch, "Tell us
what you saw."

"OK," said Maxi, wiping his mouth
with a napkin and taking a quick nervous
look around him. "I always take an
early evening walk and yesterday was no
different. I cut through the West Side
Wood and was a short way away from
the bank when I heard weird noises. I
looked up and for a second I spotted
what looked like two extra-large footballs

moving along the ground. They were only in sight for a few seconds, but I definitely saw them. I carried on my walk and then went to bed."

"That's all you've got for us?" said Itch angrily. "Two suspicious footballs?"

"It could be useful," said Buzz, getting up quickly and motioning for Itch to do the same.

"Thanks for the food," said Maxi, viewing them with darting eyes. "If you ever need more info you know where to find me."

Itch showed Maxi the *FRI, NIGHT, TOAD* note, but Maxi insisted he'd never seen it before and that he never cooked so it couldn't have been written by him.

"What do you think about Maxi?" asked Buzz, when the Fleatectives had stepped outside Flakey's.

"He likes eating," replied Itch. "I wish I could have had a few bites of those chalk fritters."

"No!" sighed Buzz. "I mean about his information. If he was so near the bank at the time of the robbery that makes him a prime suspect."

"You think he was making up the stuff about seeing those two moving footballs to put us off his scent?" asked Itch.

"Maybe," nodded Buzz, "but if he was telling the truth, I know where we should head next."

After crossing over a small stream and passing two worms that were arguing about their lack of Bug Notes, the Fleatectives neared Larva Town's Open Field. There stood a lean adult cricket and a bunch of cricket kids.

But Buzz and Itch hadn't even reached the fence around the field when something flew through the air, bashed straight into the Fleatectives and knocked them both flat out.

Can you find the
eight hidden stars?

Answers at the back of the book

CHAPTER 5

"Ow, that hurt!" mumbled Buzz as he slowly came round.

"Am I dead?" murmured Itch dreamily.

The Fleatectives opened their eyes and found a small group of child crickets staring down at them in fascination.

"Which one of you fired a nectar-powered bomb at us?" demanded Itch, struggling to his feet.

"It wasn't a bomb," replied one of the kids. "It was that."

Buzz got up. He and Itch looked to where the kid was pointing and saw a football lying next to them on the grass.

"It's so clever how they disguise bombs these days," said Itch.

"Er ... it's actually a football," said Buzz, picking it up and bouncing it on the ground.

"Well, who kicked it at us?" demanded Itch.

The cricket kids turned round and looked at the adult cricket who was wearing an old green tracksuit, and a whistle round his neck. He was standing at the side of the field, looking angry.

"I'm Fleb, the Larva Town youth football coach," chirruped the tracksuited cricket, "and you're interrupting my football training. Kids, get back here now!"

FLEATASTIC FACT:

Lots of people think crickets give out messages. A cricket chirrup in Brazil is thought to mean that rain is coming, while a loud cricket chirrup in Barbados is supposed to mean that you or someone near to you is going to get a big pile of money soon!

The cricket kids gulped and raced back to Fleb.

"He must be the cash burglar," hissed Itch under his breath. "He kicked the ball at us to try to scare us away and stop us from asking him fleatastically clever questions."

"Well, he hasn't scared us away, has he?" whispered Buzz, "so let's ask him those questions."

The Fleatectives strolled over to the pitch and stopped when they reached Fleb. All of the young crickets were now running around the field with mini footballs, doing flicks and tricks with their many legs, and headers with their antennae.

"Do you normally fire football rockets at world-famous crime-crushers?" demanded Itch.

"It was an accident," said Fleb sourly.

"What do you know about the two

extra-large footballs seen lurking near Larva Town Bank at the time of the robbery yesterday?" asked Buzz.

"I haven't seen anything like that. Those are the only footballs in town," replied Fleb, pointing to the ones the child crickets were playing with.

"And why should we believe that?" said Itch.

"Now listen here, you two unsporting bags of laziness!" hissed Fleb. "When I say I haven't seen any oversized footballs, I mean I haven't seen them. So if there's nothing else you want to ask, I suggest you hop off!"

Itch raised himself to his full height, until his head almost reached Fleb's waist. "Well, we'll be searching every blade of grass round here," he said firmly.

So the Fleatectives did. They looked all over the training pitch, in the changing rooms and inside Fleb's bags. But there were no big footballs and no sign of any Bug Notes. Before they left, they asked him about the *FRI, NIGHT, TOAD* note. "I'm a VEGETARIAN!" he snarled. "I have never and will never eat any type of toad however juicy it may be!"

He scowled at the Fleatectives as they walked away from the field.

"Fleb's tracksuit and those footballs looked really old," said Itch. "He might have stolen the money to get new stuff. He could be hiding the cash some place."

"Maybe," replied Buzz, "but we haven't got a shred of evidence against him, or against Snoop and Maxi."

"We're not making any progress on this case are we?" said Itch miserably.

"I don't agree," replied Buzz. "We've found some clues; we just don't know what they mean yet. I say we go back to the bank and take another look."

"But we've already checked it out," complained Itch. "There were no Bug Notes and no claw or feeler prints anywhere."

"I know," said Buzz, "but we weren't there for a very long time, so we may have missed something."

"OK," sighed Itch. "Let's give it a go."

A short while later the Fleatectives made it to the bank. Van Punchem had left the door open. After all, what was the point of locking it when there was no money left inside? Buzz and Itch got down on their knees and started crawling round the vault.

"This is boring," moaned Itch, "and my knees are getting sore."

They crawled over bits of dust and brick, and past a few white dots that definitely weren't from Bug Notes.

"These look interesting," murmured Buzz, crouching down and looking at the dots. "I wonder where they come from."

"They're probably small bits of paper

from the *FRI, NIGHT, TOAD* message
we found," sighed Itch.

"But I think they're moving," said Buzz.
"Let me take a look," said Itch.
"You'll be looking at nothing but the
walls of a prison cell!" cried a voice as
handcuffs were suddenly snapped round
the Fleatectives' claws.

Can you find the missing words?

```
Q U D H A D K Z T Q I M
A P O B S T H Q R T D A
X J E D A C L E E J U X
K M S T O L E N L R I I
T E T E S B E A S Y Z Z
E Q R I T C H V R N A O
K J J I B O S H P S V T
C A R G Z I N M U I G W
I O B U Z Z A G A C F I
R W E Z M L H U U A E Q
C V F L E A S P T B Z B
X R K Y V B A N K X Z A
```

BUZZ	MAXI
ITCH	BANK
STOLEN	CRICKET
FLEAS	BUG NOTES

Answers at the back of the book

CHAPTER 6

"GET OFF ME!" screamed Itch, trying to wriggle out of the handcuffs.

"HOW DARE YOU!" yelled Buzz.

"One, I will not get off you, and two, I do dare!" said the voice. The Fleatectives heard a match being lit and a moment later the small light of a candle appeared in the darkness.

"SHERIFF BLATT?" blurted out Buzz and Itch.

The cockroach's face was lit up by the candlelight, his shadow stretching across the wall behind him. "That's right," nodded Blatt with a satisfied grin.

"I knew you were terrible at catching criminals but now I can see you are criminals yourselves!"

"What are you talking about?" gasped Itch. "I've never stolen anything … well, apart from a few biscuit crumbs from my cousin Gilbert's biscuit tin."

"We're not the criminals!" cried Buzz. "We're here to find clues, which is a lot more than you've done so far on this case!"

"You can talk all you like," snapped the sheriff, "but when I heard voices inside the vault I knew they must belong to the burglars. You've come back here to see if you missed any Bug Notes or to cover your tracks, or to do any of the other things that robbers do. I know a guilty insect when I see one!"

"But, Sheriff Blatt—" protested Itch.

"SILENCE!" shouted Blatt. "I don't want to hear another word. You're coming with me."

"This is SO frustrating!" whispered Itch as Blatt prodded them forwards on the path to the Sheriff's office.

"I'm sure those white dots are connected to the crime," said Buzz. "I think we need just one or two more clues and then everything will fit into place."

"We won't find any more clues if it's up to Blatt," groaned Itch.

When they arrived at the office, the sheriff asked them to empty their claw pockets. Buzz had nothing in his. Itch had a chewed-up football card, a pack of grit chewing gum, a mini-Goo-bix cube and a half-eaten mud doughnut.

Next, Blatt led them towards his barred jail cell, shoved them inside and slammed the door. It shut with a loud *clang*.

"You've got this all wrong!" snarled Buzz. "We're innocent. The guilty insect or insects will be laughing their heads off.

We've found some suspects. If you just listen to us we'll tell you who they are and everything else we know."

"You were caught crawling around the crime scene," replied Blatt. "You haven't got a leg to stand on."

"Actually, we do have legs to stand on," said Itch, "Buzz has got his legs and I've got my legs, so between us we've got. . ."

"You were there and that's enough for me!" snapped Blatt.

"Please, Sheriff Blatt!" wailed Itch.

"You're making a terrible mistake!" cried Buzz.

But the Sheriff untied their handcuffs, locked the cell door with a huge silver key, then left the room and turned on his giant TV in the room next door.

"Oh, this is just great!" groaned Itch. "We're stuck here till the end of our days."

FLEATASTIC FACT:

If fleas stay in the same place for a long time and don't use too much energy, they can last one hundred days without eating!

"If the sheriff thinks we did it, the real criminals will have plenty of time to get away with the money," said Buzz.

"If they've taken the money out of Larva Town, maybe someone will see it and report it to us," said Itch hopefully.

"We can't rely on other insects," said Buzz. "We have to crack this case ourselves."

"OK," said Itch. "How about we pretend that we're the crooks? What's the first thing we'd do after stealing the cash?"

"We'd probably hide it somewhere for a few days – you know, wait until all of the fuss had died down a bit."

The theme tune of the police show *Insect Crime-Busters* suddenly blared out from Blatt's TV, interrupting their conversation.

"Tonight's show is all about the gruesome bee gang that knocked people out with toadstool poison before stealing all of their insect jewellery," announced the presenter. "The toadstools they used were some of the most dangerous ones known to insects."

As these words were being broadcast, Buzz was looking through the cell bars at a calendar stuck on to a wall. A thought suddenly zipped into his brain.

"Itch," he said, "I think I may have just had a light-bulb moment."

"We don't need a light bulb," said Itch, "this place is perfectly well lit."

"No," sighed Buzz, "I mean I've just had an incredible idea."

"What is it?" asked Itch.

"You know we found the *FRI, NIGHT, TOAD* note in the bank?" said Buzz.

Itch nodded.

"It was ripped so we couldn't read the whole message, but maybe it isn't to do with frying toads at all. Maybe the 'Fri' stands for Friday, the 'night' means night and the 'toad' means toadstools?"

"Toadstools?" said Itch. "How can toadstools be related to the theft or the storing of the money?"

"There are two toadstool speakers in Larva Town Square," said Buzz, his face suddenly lighting up. "What if the burglars stole the cash, stashed it in the toadstools and decided to move it on Friday night?"

"When is Friday night?" asked Itch.

"Now," replied Buzz. "We have to get out of here immediately. We may be too late."

"Leave it to me," said Itch. He threw himself on the ground and yelled, "I

THINK I'M DYING!" at the top of his voice.

A few seconds later, an angry Sheriff Blatt appeared round the corner and stood in front of the cell.

Itch was twisting around on the floor and clutching his abdomen. "Help me, Sheriff," croaked Itch. "I'm in terrible pain. I need a doctor immediately."

"I know a lot about first aid," said Blatt proudly. "I'm sure there'll be no need for a doctor."

He pulled out the key, opened the door and strode over to Itch. As he was kneeling down to look at the patient, Buzz shoved him on to the ground.

"OOOF!" cried the sheriff furiously, but he was too late to stop his prisoners from rushing past him. "STOP RIGHT NOW!" he bellowed, but the Fleatectives were already out of the jail and racing towards Larva Town Square.

Which Buzz is the odd one out?

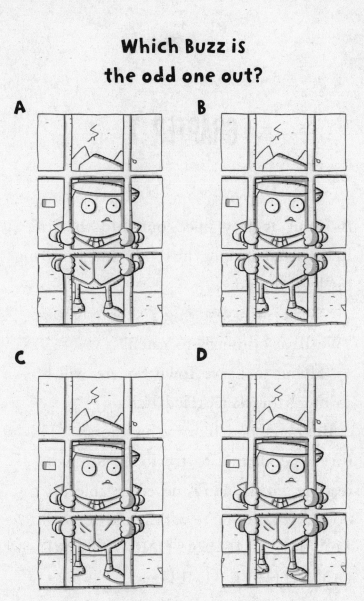

A **B**

C **D**

Answers at the back of the book

CHAPTER 7

As soon as they piled out into the street, Itch started shaking his body and throwing his legs around.

"What are you doing?" shouted Buzz. "We have criminals to catch!"

"Flying to Larva Town Square will be so much quicker," cried Itch.

Buzz grabbed Itch by his thorax. "This isn't a good time to try to fly for two reasons. Firstly, you'll never be able to do it because you're a flea, and secondly, YOU'RE TIME-WASTING AND WE DON'T HAVE TIME!"

Itch stopped, sighed deeply and began

racing after his crime-crushing partner.

"What if they've already moved the cash?" panted Itch, as the Fleatectives sprinted down a wide road.

"If they have we'll probably never find the money," replied Buzz, "but we've got to try."

On they raced, their flea hearts beating like a rock star wasp's drum kit.

"Which of our suspects do you think it is?" asked Itch. "Snoop, Maxi or Fleb?"

"It could be any of them," said Buzz, "and in a few minutes we'll hopefully discover the truth."

Skidding round a corner they burst into Larva Town Square. At the far end they could see the two massive toadstools standing on either side of the town square stage. They could also see a shadowy figure moving around next to one toadstool, and another shadowy figure moving around next to the other toadstool. On the ground nearby were two large bags.

"They must be the robbers," hissed Buzz, pointing at the figures.

"There's *two* of them!" whispered Itch.

"It could be Snoop and Maxi, or Snoop and Fleb, or Maxi and Fleb, or Snoop, Maxi and Fleb if one of them is waiting in a getaway vehicle."

"Let's surprise them," said Buzz.

The two Fleatectives crept forwards, keeping their eyes on the toadstools, the two moving figures and the two bags on the ground. As they got nearer, the figures became less shadowy and started to look like two giant footballs.

"Fleb lied to us and Maxi told us the truth," growled Itch. "There *are* two extra-large footballs in Larva Town! Fleb must be one of the crooks!"

But when they were only a very short distance away, the Fleatectives suddenly saw that while the figures did have markings on them, they were not footballs. . .

They were ladybirds!

"Lilac and Mauve!" exclaimed Itch, gaping open-mouthed at the two figures.

The ladybirds were grabbing huge piles of Bug Notes from the hollowed-out insides of the toadstools and stuffing them into their two fashionable handbags.

They spun round when they heard Itch's voice.

"So you're the bank robbers!" gasped Buzz.

"Not you two Flea-fectives, or whatever silly name you call yourselves!" snapped Violet.

"It's actually Fleatectives," answered Itch. "So that's why you were standing at the end of that tunnel," said Buzz. "You'd just come out of it. You'd just robbed the bank."

"But where was the money?" asked Itch.

"It was stuffed into these handbags, which you so kindly admired!" snarled Mauve, pointing to the two bags on the ground.

"And there's nothing you puny fleas can do about it!" added Lilac with a triumphant shout.

"It all makes sense now," said Buzz. "Those white dots on the floor of the vault weren't bits of paper – they were aphids, weren't they?"

"What, you mean those little creatures that ladybirds eat?" asked Itch.

"Absolutely," nodded Buzz. "They must have brought them along as a bank-robbing snack and then dropped some by mistake."

"Robbing all of that money was tough work," scowled Mauve. "We had to take some kind of meal."

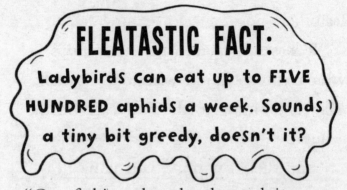

FLEATASTIC FACT:
Ladybirds can eat up to FIVE HUNDRED aphids a week. Sounds a tiny bit greedy, doesn't it?

"Our fashion shop has been doing really badly," said Lilac. "If we didn't get our hands on a lot of cash pretty soon, the business would have collapsed and we'd have lost everything."

"So you thought it was OK to steal all of the money from Larva Town Bank?" questioned Itch sharply. "To save *your* business, you were happy to take money away from everyone else?"

"Who cares about anyone else?" declared Lilac. "Our fashion store is the best shop in town. We would do anything to save it, even if it means letting all of the other shops get closed down."

"Well we've caught you red-handed – or, rather, red-backed with black spots," said Itch. "You're both in BIG trouble."

"The only ones getting into trouble will be you two," sneered Mauve.

With a high-pitched shriek, the ladybirds charged at the Fleatectives. Lilac grabbed Itch. Mauve grabbed Buzz. They lifted the fleas up by their antennae and threw them towards the two hollowed-out toadstools. Itch landed inside the right one and Buzz landed inside the left one.

An instant later Lilac and Mauve grabbed the two toadstool roofs that were lying on the ground and hoisted them up into the air.

"Let me out of here!" demanded Itch.

"You won't be going anywhere, ever again!" shouted Lilac.

"And no one will hear your cries from in there!" added Mauve.

The ladybirds flung the toadstool roofs straight at the toadstool bodies. In a few seconds the Fleatectives would be trapped inside for ever.

Can you fit all the missing words into this puzzle?

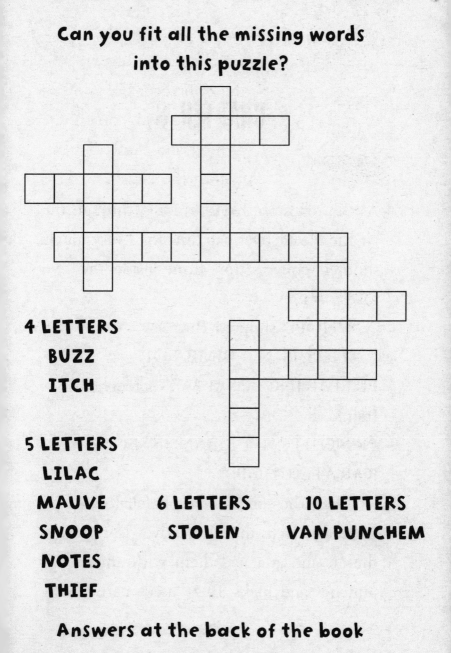

4 LETTERS
BUZZ
ITCH

5 LETTERS
LILAC
MAUVE
SNOOP
NOTES
THIEF

6 LETTERS
STOLEN

10 LETTERS
VAN PUNCHEM

Answers at the back of the book

CHAPTER 8

As the toadstool roofs whizzed through the air, the Fleatectives had time for a very quick, shouted conversation from inside the two toadstools.

"CHOP!" shouted Buzz.

"THIS IS NO TIME FOR PREPARING A SALAD!" screeched Itch.

"NO, ITCH. I MEAN INSECT KARATE CHOP!"

When the toadstool roofs fell towards Buzz and Itch, the Fleatectives leapt into the air and attacked them with amazing punches and kicks. Buzz used martial arts

moves he'd learnt over the years. Itch made them up as he went along. With a series of jumps and thwacks, the roofs were cut to pieces.

Lilac and Mauve grabbed their cash-stuffed handbags and started to run, but toadstool chunks rained down, pinning them to the ground.

Buzz and Itch sprung out of the toadstools and gazed in delight at the two trapped criminal ladybirds.

At that second, Sheriff Blatt arrived on the scene, looking furious. "Now I've got you!" he shouted at the Fleatectives, bringing out his handcuffs and glaring at them.

"We're not the crooks!" yelled Itch. "Those two on the ground are the villains. They robbed the bank, hid the money in these toadstools and were about to leave town with all of our Bug Notes in their fashion handbags."

"We were going to set up a brand-new fashion store in another town," groaned Lilac.

"It was going to be the most wonderful store in the entire insect world," whined Mauve.

"And they'd have got away with it if we hadn't escaped from your cell and rushed here," said Buzz.

"That's exactly what I planned to happen," said Blatt, quickly changing his story. "I knew those two ladybirds were behind all of this. I wanted you to escape from my cell so that you would lead me to them."

"But if you knew it was Lilac and Mauve, why didn't you arrest them earlier?" demanded Itch.

"A great criminal-catching insect never acts too quickly. He lets the clues build up in his mind and then he makes his move."

"But you didn't have any clues," pointed out Itch. "You had it all wrong because you arrested us and we had nothing to do with it!"

At that second Van Punchem raced into the square and made a beeline for the little group. His eyes enlarged by at least three sizes as he feasted his eyes on what was inside the handbags.

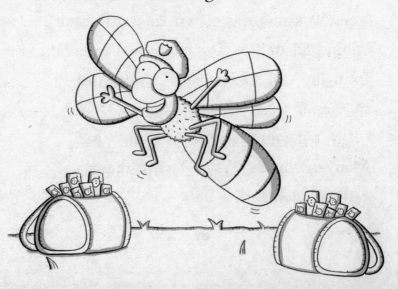

"The stolen money!" he exclaimed, grabbing both handbags and holding them as if they were newborn dragonfly babies. "I knew I'd find it!"

"Hey, we found it!" snapped Itch.

"Another brilliantly solved case for the Larva Town Sheriff," beamed Blatt.

"I can't believe I've got all of the bank's money back," grinned Van Punchem. "I am going to make security SO much better at the bank now. I'll put in solid metal floors and doors. I'll hire two extra security guards. I'll block out all of the windows. Why, I might even sleep inside the building each night."

"Make sure you take a sleeping bag," said Itch. "It might get a bit cold."

Van Punchem smiled gratefully and went on his way with the two precious handbags.

"Right," said Blatt, kicking aside some toadstool chunks, then snapping handcuffs on Lilac and Mauve. "It's off to the town jail for you."

He turned to face Buzz and Itch. "In future, can you leave the crime solving to me?" he said.

"Aren't you going to apologize for locking us up?" asked Itch.

"I didn't lock you up," said the sheriff, "I was merely the insect who turned the key."

"You're selfish, cruel and mean, Fleatectives!" shrieked Lilac. "We'd be miles away from here if it wasn't for you two crime-crushers."

"We'll get back to our new fashion shop eventually," snarled Mauve, "and when we do, you'll be laughing on the other side of your insect sweaters."

"Yeah, yeah," said Itch, "save it for your prison cell."

"I love a successful case," said Blatt, giving the Fleatectives a superior smile and dragging the ladybirds off in the direction of his office.

"I can't believe Blatt has done it again," moaned Itch. "We did all of the legwork and he says he cracked the crime."

"I know," nodded Buzz, patting Itch on the abdomen. "But we know the truth and that's the most important thing."

By the time the Fleatectives got back to Lambert, Buzz had managed to convince Itch that Sheriff Blatt taking credit for solving the case wasn't the end of the world.

"We caught two criminal ladybirds and now Larva Town has all of its money back," Buzz told Lambert.

"We're getting good at this Fleatective thing, aren't we?" smiled Itch.

Lambert opened one eye. "It sounds like you did very well out there," she said.

"Thanks," smiled Itch. "It's nice to know that someone appreciates us!"

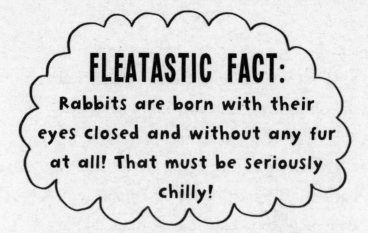

FLEATASTIC FACT:
Rabbits are born with their eyes closed and without any fur at all! That must be seriously chilly!

The Fleatectives got cosy in their beds and lay there looking up at the inky black sky and the pale moon. Buzz closed his eyes and started drifting off. Itch lay there for a while wondering about their next case. Would it be scary? Would it dangerous? Would there be chalk fritters to eat? He got more comfortable and a few moments later, both Fleatectives were fast asleep.

Can you spot the eight differences between the two images?

Answers on the next page

Here are the
answers to our
Fleatective puzzles

Page 12

1. CRUSTMAN
2. BUZZ AND ITCH
3. BUG NOTES
4. VAN PUNCHEM
5. PAINTED LADY
6. LARVA TOWN
   BANK

Page 39

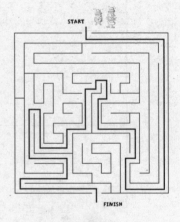

Page 28

Path 'B'

Page 53

Page 63

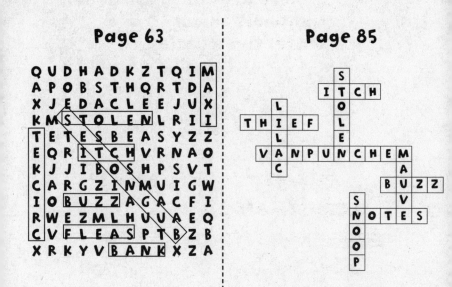

Page 85

Page 75

Buzz 'D'

Page 97

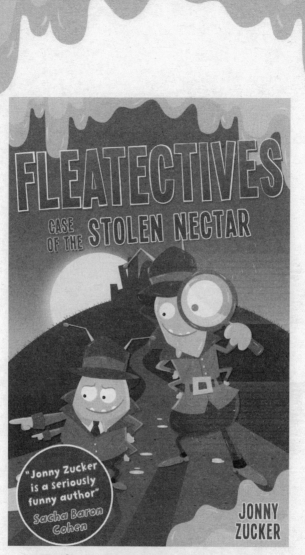

All the nectar in Larva Town
has gone missing!
The West Side bees say it's
the East Side bees, but are
either of them really to blame?
It's up to the Fleatectives
to find the culprit.

Larva Town is in darkness!
Someone has stolen the
glow-worms and without
them the insect town is in
danger from thieves and crooks.
Luckily, the Fleatectives
are on the case!

The mayor of Larva Town
has been kidnapped!
Without him in charge, the insects
of the town will be out of control.
Can the Fleatectives find the
mayor before it's too late?

Larva Town's
#1 Crime Crushers